THE VERY CRANKY BEAR

To Tom and Sam. NB.

Text and illustrations copyright © 2008 by Nicholas Bland

All rights reserved. Published by Orchard Books, an imprint of Scholastic Inc.,
Publishers since 1920. ORCHARD BOOKS and design are registered trademarks of
Watts Publishing Group, Ltd., used under license. SCHOLASTIC and associated
logos are trademarks and/or registered trademarks of Scholastic Inc.

No part of this publication may be reproduced, stored in a retrieval system, or
transmitted in any form or by any means, electronic, mechanical, photocopying,
recording, or otherwise, without written permission of the publisher. For
information regarding permission, write to Orchard Books, Scholastic Inc.,
Permissions Department, 557 Broadway, New York, NY 10012.

The Very Cranky Bear was originally published in Australia
by Scholastic Australia Pty Limited in 2008.

Library of Congress Cataloging-in-Publication Data

Bland, Nick, 1973- author.
The very cranky bear / Nick Bland. — First American edition.   pages cm.
"Originally published in Australia by Scholastic Australia Pty Limited in 2008."
Summary: On a cold, rainy day in the jungle, four animal friends hide in a cave
to play, but unexpectedly meet a very cranky bear trying to nap.
ISBN 978-0-545-61269-2
1. Bears—Juvenile fiction. 2. Animals—Juvenile fiction. 3. Anger—Juvenile
fiction. 4. Friendship—Juvenile fiction. 5. Stories in rhyme. [1. Stories in
rhyme. 2. Bears—Fiction. 3. Jungle animals—Fiction. 4. Anger—Fiction.
5. Friendship—Fiction] I. Title.   PZ8.3.B59714Ve 2014   [E]—dc23
2013035028

10 9 8 7 6 5 4 3 2 1   14 15 16 17 18

Printed in Malaysia   108
First American edition, August 2014

Typeset in Bitstream Cooper BT and Volcano King.

U.S. edition designed by Chelsea C. Donaldson

THE VERY CRANKY BEAR

NICK BLAND

Orchard Books • An Imprint of Scholastic Inc. • New York

In the Jingle Jangle Jungle on a cold and rainy day,
four little friends found a perfect place to play.

Moose had marvelous antlers, and Lion, a golden mane.
Zebra had fantastic stripes, and Sheep . . . well, Sheep was plain.

None of them had noticed that someone else was there.

Sleeping in that cave was a very cranky . . .

BEAR!

"RoAAAAR," went the cranky bear,

"RoAR, RoAR, RoAR!"

He gnashed his teeth and stomped his feet
and chased them out the door.

So in the Jingle Jangle Jungle on a cold and rainy day,
four little friends had nowhere warm to play.

"Wait a minute," said Zebra,
as she scratched her furry chin.
"Maybe if we cheered him up,
he'd let us come back in."

"If I did not have stripes," said Zebra,
"I'd be cranky, too.
We should give that bear some stripes.
That's what we should do."

"Stripes are silly," Moose complained,
"especially on a bear.
My antlers always cheer me up.
Let's give that bear a pair."

"No, no, no, no, no," said Lion,
"antlers are a bore!
A golden mane like mine," he said,
"would cheer him up for sure."

So Zebra fetched a can of mud,
and Lion, some grass of gold.

Moose got two big branches,
and Sheep . . . well, Sheep got cold.

Sheep was getting worried.
"They've been eaten up for sure!"

And then, from inside the cave,
there came a very cranky . . .

"ROAAAAR!"

Zebra, Lion, and Moose ran out, and Bear was right behind them.
They hid behind the bushes, where they hoped he wouldn't find them.

"Why is he still cranky? He's got antlers, stripes, and a mane.
Before we gave him those," Lion said, "he looked so very plain!"

As Bear stormed back inside the cave,
he turned and roared at Sheep.

"ALL I REALLY WANT," he said,

"IS A QUIET PLACE TO SLEEP!"

So she fetched a pair of clippers, and she sheared off half her wool.

She stuffed it in a cotton bag until the bag was full.

She tiptoed back inside the cave. "Excuse me, Bear," she said.
"Would you like a pillow for underneath your head?"

"Well, thank you very much," said Bear, and soon he fell asleep.
Maybe he was dreaming of a plain but thoughtful sheep.